The Golden Christmas Tree

By JAN WAHL

Illustrated by
LEONARD WEISGARD

To Joe and Andrea

All was hushed in the forest
for the animals' Christmas.
The elephant brought a great fir tree
from far away.

A red cardinal flew through the trees,
carrying the news—
"The fir is here, the fir is here."

The llamas and the goats,
who were slow of thinking,
thought,
"We already have our fur."

The wolf helped the red deer,
  whose antlers caught
      on low-hanging branches.

  Silently they walked together,
joined by the badger and
a family of foxes—
guided by bats who whistled soft carols.

Squirrels whispered stories
of the time the first Christmas came,
announced by a ringing
like clear crystal bells.

Now, as it happened before,
the lion lay down with the lamb.

The animals gathered, one by one....
There was no
growling, howling, meowling,
anywhere.

It was
hushed in the forest,
hushed,
   hushed,
      hushed,
         hushed.

The kangaroos picked cones and leaves
to hang on the branches.

The tiger
strung
berries.

The antelope chewed the grass,
making a smooth lawn
for the fir.

The baboons painted pinecones carefully.

The monkeys put the ornaments on.

And the giraffe laid, at the top, a star.

Then the tree was ready.
The animals gathered
in the silvery moonlight.
The raccoon lit the lights.
Darkness fell, but

no one moved.

Now, up in the sky, there appeared
a great constellation of bright shiny stars.

The bear said he was sure it was
a large and little bear.

The tiger was sure it was
a large and little tiger.

Then a delicate golden glitter flashed—

and each in that moment
made his quiet wish.

The cardinal's brothers and sisters dropped
walnuts and apricots, chestnuts and plums,
with a rustle of whirring wings.

The beautiful fir stood flickering all night.
And they danced—
        they danced—
                they danced
                        until it was light of morning.